Excuse Me, Dad

An Ivy and Mack story

Contents

Written by Rebecca Colby

Illustrated by Gustavo Mazali

with Martyn Cain

Collins

Who's in this story?

Listen and say 

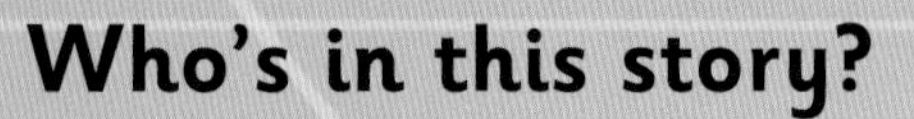

 Download the audio at www.collins.co.uk/839728

Mr Jackson
Ms Lemon

Chapter 1 Time for work

Ivy came home from school with a **letter**. She gave it to Dad. Dad read, "*Take your child to work day.*"

"What does that mean?" asked Ivy.

"It means you can come to work with me. You can learn about my **job** and help me," said Dad. "Would you like that?"

"Ooh, yes please!" said Ivy.

Mack looked up at Dad. "What do you do at work?" he asked.

"Well, I **teach** the piano. And I talk to my students about their homework," answered Dad.

"Are you their favourite teacher?" asked Mack.

"Of course, he is!" said Ivy.

The next day, Ivy was ready to go to work with Dad.

"It's 8 o'clock. Come on, Dad! It's time to go."

Dad took Ivy to work and Mum took Mack to school. They all waved.

"Can I go to work with you, Mum?" asked Mack.

"Yes, but not today!" said Mum.

Chapter 2 This is where I work

Dad worked in a very big **building**. He pointed to a window. "That's my room," he said. "But let's go to my classroom **first**."

They went to Dad's classroom. "This is where I teach my lessons," he said.

"Wow!" said Ivy. "Look at all these pianos and computers!"

Outside the classroom, they **met** a tall woman with grey hair.

"This is Ms Lemon. She teaches music here, too."

Dad and Ms Lemon talked. And they talked. And they talked. It was very **boring**.

"Excuse me, Dad. Can I see your room?" said Ivy.

Ms Lemon went back to her room.
"Let's do some work now," said Ivy.
"What do we do first?"

Dad took her to the café. "I want a cup of coffee first," he said.

After his coffee, Dad took Ivy to his room.
"Here we are," he said.

"We can start work!" said Ivy.

"Yes, we can."

Then, a man **knocked** on the door.
"Hello, Jim," said Dad. Jim and Dad talked.
And they talked. And they talked.
It was very boring.

"Is this what you do at work? Do you only drink coffee and talk to people?" asked Ivy.

Dad laughed. "No," he said. "I use my computer to write lessons and **send** messages. I teach my students how to play the piano and I listen to them **practise**!"

A student came to the door. “Can I talk to you about my homework please, Mr West?” he asked.

“Excuse me, Dad, but what can I do?” asked Ivy.

“You can **water** the plants,” said Dad.

Ivy watered Dad's plants. Dad and the student talked and talked.

Chapter 3 Ivy waits for Dad

And Ivy **waited** … and waited. "This is boring," she thought. "Excuse me, Dad," she said, but Dad didn't hear her.

"Oh dear!" thought Ivy. "Dad isn't doing any work. How can I help him?" Then she had an idea. She could **tidy** his desk.

Ivy sat down in front of Dad's computer and moved the mouse.

Dad had lots of messages. "Oh dear!" thought Ivy. Then she had an idea. "I can answer these!"

Ivy wrote Dad's message to Mr Jackson quickly. "Good," she said happily.

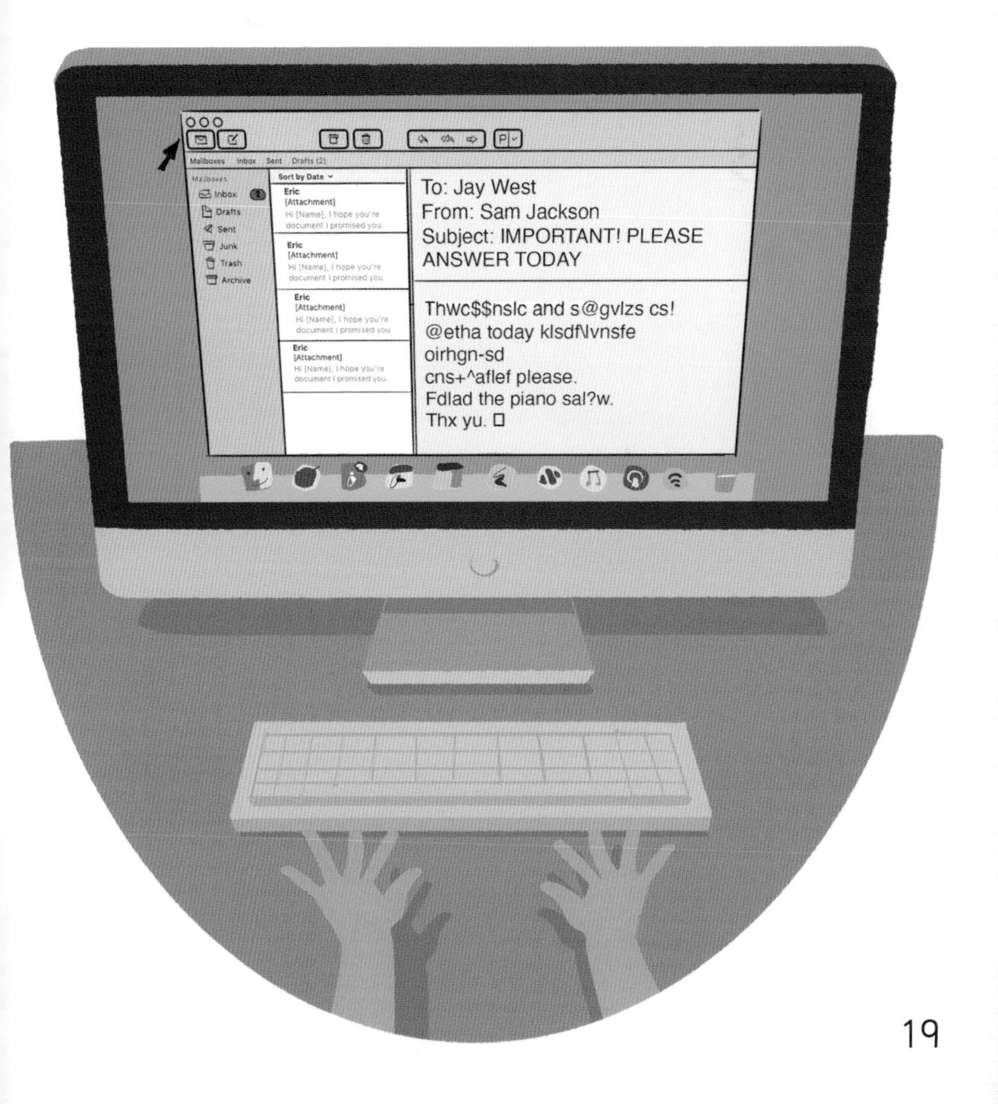

Ivy wrote lots of messages for Dad on the computer. Then she looked in Dad's desk. Chocolate!

She ate one square of chocolate ... two squares of chocolate ...

Chapter 4 What did you do?

Dad came back into the room. “What did you do?” he asked.

“I did all your work,” she said. “Look!”

For the first time all day, Dad stopped talking. He didn’t know what to say.

Ivy smiled and gave Dad some chocolate.

“What can I do now?” she asked.

"You can have a **break**," said Dad. He cleaned the floor.

"It's OK, Dad. I'm not tired. Your work is easy," said Ivy.

Dad found his papers. Then he ate some more chocolate.

Ivy looked at Dad's books.
"Dad! The phone!" she said. "Shall I answer it?"

"No, Ivy. It's OK, thanks," said Dad.

Dad answered the phone. "Hello, Ms Lemon," he said. "Yes, I'm looking for that paper now."

A man came to the door and Ivy opened it. "Hello," she said. "I'm Mr West's daughter, Ivy."

"I'm Mr Jackson," said the man.

"Oh! Did you get your message?" said Ivy. "I wrote it for Dad."

"It's *Take your child to work day*," Dad told Mr Jackson.

"Ah …" said Mr Jackson. "So the message …"

"Was from Ivy," said Dad.

"Your face!" said Mr Jackson.

"Oh, no!" said Dad.

"Oh, yes!" said Ivy.

They all laughed.

Chapter 5 The music lesson

"What can we do now?" Ivy asked.

"Let's have lunch and then I have a lesson to teach," said Dad. "You can watch."

"Great!" said Ivy.

Dad played the piano to his students.

“That was **amazing**!” said a student.

“Thanks, Mr West,” said a second student.

“Your dad is great!” a student said to Ivy.

Ivy clapped and clapped.

At home Mum asked, “How was your day at work, Ivy?”

“It was great,” said Ivy. “I did Dad’s work and I didn’t make any mistakes!”

“Was Dad the favourite teacher?”
Mack asked Ivy.

“Yes, he was,” said Ivy. “Dad’s very good at his job.”

Mini-dictionary

Listen and read 

amazing (adjective) Something that is **amazing** is very good.

boring (adjective) Something that is **boring** is not very interesting or exciting.

break (noun) A **break** is a short period of time when you stop what you are doing.

building (noun) A **building** has walls and a roof, for example a house or a school.

first (adverb) If you do something **first**, you do it before you do anything else.

job (noun) A **job** is the work that someone does to earn money.

knock (verb) If you **knock** on something, you hit it hard with your hand to make a noise.

letter (noun) A **letter** is a message that someone writes on paper to give to another person.

met (past tense of meet) (verb) If you **meet** someone you know, you see them and speak to them.

outside (preposition) Someone or something that is **outside** a place is not in it, but very close to it.

practise (verb) If you **practise** something, you do it a lot so that you can do it better.

send (verb) If you **send** a message, you make it go to someone, for example on the computer.

teach (verb) If someone **teaches** you something, they help you learn about it or show you how to do it.

tidy (verb) If you **tidy** a place, you make it nice by putting things where they have to go.

wait (verb) If you **wait**, you spend time in a place, usually doing nothing, before something happens.

water (verb) If you water a plant, you pour water into the soil around it.

1 Look and order the story

2 Listen and say  

Download a reading guide for parents and teachers at www.collins.co.uk/839728

Collins

Published by Collins
An imprint of HarperCollins*Publishers*
Westerhill Road
Bishopbriggs
Glasgow
G64 2QT

HarperCollins*Publishers*
1st Floor, Watermarque Building
Ringsend Road
Dublin 4
Ireland

William Collins' dream of knowledge for all began with the publication of his first book in 1819.

A self-educated mill worker, he not only enriched millions of lives, but also founded a flourishing publishing house. Today, staying true to this spirit, Collins books are packed with inspiration, innovation and practical expertise. They place you at the centre of a world of possibility and give you exactly what you need to explore it.

10 9 8 7 6 5 4 3 2

ISBN 978-0-00-839728-9

www.collins.co.uk/elt

British Library Cataloguing in Publication Data

A catalogue record for this publication is available from the British Library.

Author: Rebecca Colby
Lead illustrator: Gustavo Mazali (Beehive)
Copy illustrator: Martyn Cain (Beehive)
Series editor: Rebecca Adlard
Commissioning editor: Zoë Clarke
Publishing manager: Lisa Todd
Product managers: Jennifer Hall and Caroline Green
In-house editor: Alma Puts Keren
Project manager: Emily Hooton
Editor: Deborah Friedland
Proofreaders: Natalie Murray and Michael Lamb
Cover designer: Kevin Robbins
Typesetter: 2Hoots Publishing Services Ltd
Audio produced by id audio, London
Reading guide author: Julie Penn
Production controller: Rachel Weaver
Printed and bound by: GPS Group, Slovenia

MIX
Paper from responsible sources
FSC™ C007454

This book is produced from independently certified FSC™ paper to ensure responsible forest management.

For more information visit: **www.harpercollins.co.uk/green**

Download the audio for this book and a reading guide for parents and teachers at www.collins.co.uk/839728